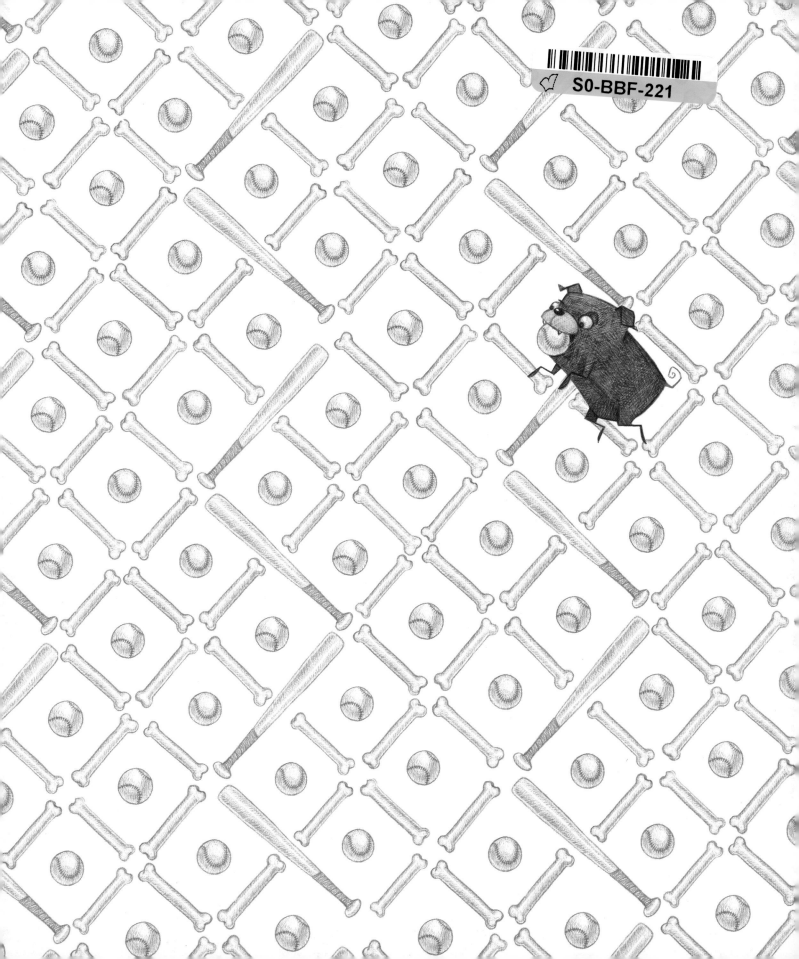

For Dickie —M.C.
For Eli —W.T.

Thanks to the all-star Ortiz family
for reading and commenting on the text.

All rights reserved. Published in the United States by Crown Books for Young Readers,
an imprint of Random House Children's Books, a division of Penguin Random House LLC, New York.

Crown and the colophon are registered trademarks of Penguin Random House LLC.

Visit us on the Web! rhcbooks.com

Educators and librarians, for a variety of teaching tools, visit us at RHTeachersLibrarians.com

Library of Congress Cataloging-in-Publication Data
Names: Cuyler, Margery, author. Terry, Will, illustrator.
Title: Bonaparte plays ball / by Margery Cuyler; illustrated by Will Terry.
Description: First edition. | New York: Crown Books for Young Readers, [2019] | Summary: Bonaparte the
skeleton and his team, the Little Monsters, face the Mighty Aliens in a monster version of the World Series.
Identifiers: LCCN 2019009361 | ISBN 978-1-9848-3047-0 (hc) | ISBN 978-1-9848-3048-7 (glb) |
ISBN 978-1-9848-3049-4 (epub)
Subjects: | CYAC: Baseball—Fiction. | Skeleton—Fiction. | Monsters—Fiction. | Extraterrestrial beings—Fiction.
Classification: LCC PZ7.C997 Bp 2020 | DDC [E]—dc23

MANUFACTURED IN CHINA

10 9 8 7 6 5 4 3 2 1

First Edition

Random House Children's Books supports the First Amendment and celebrates the right to read.

BONAPARTE
Plays Ball

by Margery Cuyler

illustrations by Will Terry

CROWN BOOKS
FOR YOUNG READERS
NEW YORK

It was the Weird Series.

Bonaparte's team, the Little Monsters,
was playing the Mighty Aliens on Saturday.
Bonaparte was a jittery jumble of bones.

What if he lost his
backbone while at bat?

What if his fetching dog, Mandible,
dropped one of his loose bones?

What if the Mighty Aliens made fun of him?

Coach Roach touched base with the team.
"You need to practice hard all week," he said.
"That's how you win."

Bonaparte whacked
and thwacked.

He hopped and bopped.

He zigged and zagged.

Finally Saturday came.

The Monsters took the field as the Mighty Aliens
clattered and scattered to their dugout.

"We'll eclipse you Monsters!" shouted Moonbob.

The Aliens were up first.
Flame Thrower clobbered
a double and charged
to second.

Eggcracker slapped a single,
scrambling to first.

The Aliens had two strikeouts before Galactic Slimer slugged a moon shot into outer space, allowing his teammates to orbit the bases on his three-run homer.

But their turn at bat ended when Mega Meteor streaked a fly ball to right field for the final out.

Now the Monsters were up.
Mummicula was the leadoff batter.

He belted a bouncer down the middle. As he hurried and
scurried toward first, his bandages ripped and he tripped.
Eggcracker ran forward and tagged him out.

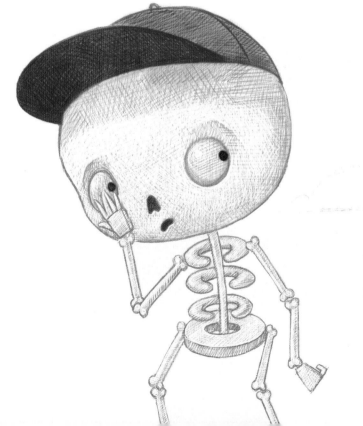

"What a bad break,"
muttered Bonaparte.

Next Franky Stein stomped to the batter's box. After two strikes, he screwed up and smacked the ball to first base.

"You're out!" yelled the umpire.

But after Zombie and Batula both hit singles, landing on first and second, Bonaparte shook his way into the batter's box.

He swung at a curveball. Strike one!

"Your head's in the clouds!" thundered Sky Boomer.

He swung at a fastball. Strike two!
"You need more meat on your bones!" shouted Mega Meteor.

A slider streaked past him.
Strike three!

"I hope this won't be a shutout," Bonaparte worried on his way back to the dugout.

The next four innings were no better.

By the end of the fifth, the score was
Mighty Aliens 5, Little Monsters 0.

"We're running rings around you!"
screeched Saturnicus.

"Let's sweep them
off the field!" said
Witchie.

Coach Roach tried to pump up the team.
"Never give up!" he said. "It ain't over till it's over!"

"Let's vaporize them!"
cried Ghostie.

"Let's squash them!"
yelled Pumpkinhead.

At the top of the sixth, the Monsters roared back to life, retiring the Aliens one by one. Bonaparte was so charged up, he could barely hold himself together.

When it was the Monsters' turn, Mummicula tried to keep his excitement under wraps as he faced down the pitcher.

Mummicula shot a line drive to left field, sliding into first before he could be tagged.

Next Franky Stein laid down a bunt, and Zombie zipped the ball to deep right field for a single. The bases were loaded!

The Little Monsters threw their mitts into the air and started cheering. "We can't be beat! We can defeat!" they chanted.

Luckily, Batula, the Monsters' cleanup hitter, was up next.

As he grabbed the bat,
Snatcher flashed garlic at him.
Batula fainted!

"Re-bolting!" cried Frankie Stein.
"Boooooo!" shouted Ghostie.
"Skullduggery!" screamed Bonaparte.
Coach Roach called for a time-out.

Suddenly Bonaparte had a brainstorm. He grabbed a
blood-orange juice box and teetered to Batula's coffin.

"We're in trouble!" yelled Bonaparte, shaking his friend awake.
"The Mighty Aliens are out for blood!" He helped Batula sit up
and poured the juice down his throat.

Batula high-fived him, then leaped up and flew to the plate.
Gripping the bat, he smashed a grand slam!

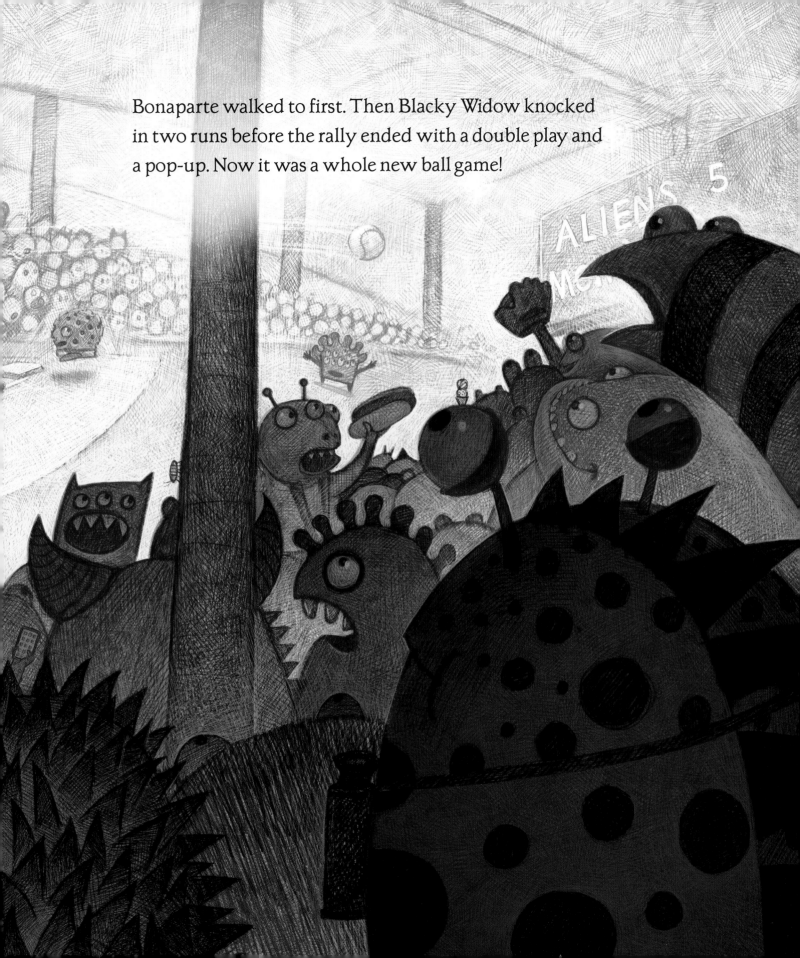

Bonaparte walked to first. Then Blacky Widow knocked in two runs before the rally ended with a double play and a pop-up. Now it was a whole new ball game!

The Monsters were still flying high during the seventh-inning stretch.

"Monsters! Monsters! Rah! Rah! Rah!
Aliens! Aliens! Ha, ha, ha!" they chanted.

But the Mighty Aliens battled back in the eighth,
with Moonbob hitting a dinger to tie the score.

It was a white-knuckle game! The score was still tied at the bottom of the ninth with just one out left after Zombie and Batula struck out.
It was all up to Bonaparte.

"Never give up, never give up, never give up!" Bonaparte repeated, quivering and shivering but gaining courage as he clickety-clacked to the plate.

Greased Lightning, the Aliens' relief pitcher, fired a slider.
Bonaparte whipped the bat around and swung for the fences.
He connected with a bone-crunching wallop!

Bonaparte's arm reached first base before
he did, but he snapped it into place.

Then he rattled around the bases, touching home plate
for the walk-off home run!
The final score was Little Monsters 7, Mighty Aliens 6.
The Little Monsters had won the game!

"You really went to bat for us!"
yelled Bonaparte's friends,
throwing him into the air.

Even the Mighty Aliens had to admit that Bonaparte was a shining star.

Bonaparte was so excited, he fell to pieces. But he didn't care. Mandible was there to put him back together.

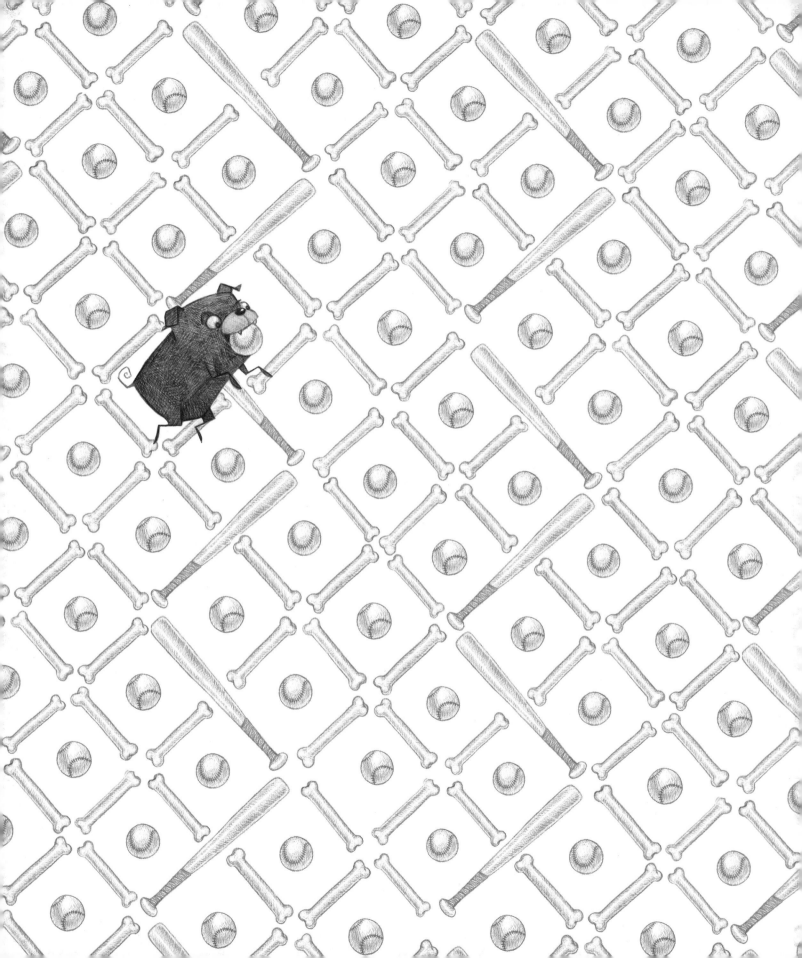